When TEDDI Met QUINN

This book belongs to

____

Written by Jackie Ahn
Illustrated by Yohan Ahn

To my little girls - J. A.

To those who showed up - Y. A.

ISBN: 978-1-7364303-0-9

The artist used markers, technical pens, and dry brush on Procreate App to create illustrations for this book.

When TEDDI Met QUINN

Teddi bear loves the park, practicing **roars** and shaking trees.

His favorite is picking berries,

and making friends

with honeybees.

See, Teddi is a bit different

from your average grizzly bear.

One day his legs stopped growing, **GRRR** it was unfair!

"Differences can bless you.

I want you to remember."

“Strength and speed are second
to a heart that’s soft and tender.”

Teddi learned from Momma

that courage is within.

So here goes our story

of how Teddi bear met Quinn.

One day in mid-spring,
as the birds began to sing,
a little girl swung too high

and went flying off her swing!

She landed in a pond filled with ooey-gooey mud.
But not before her fall made a
BOOM crash-tastic THUD.

The other kids stood watching.

Before anyone could sigh,

charging over
came the
shyest bear.

"I'll help you, I'll really try!"

Teddi plopped in the murky pool,

while tears filled Quinn's eyes.

Courage swelled Teddi’s little heart,
equal to twice its size.

He wiggled his way across the stinky, slimy sludge.

When all of the sudden, “Oh no!” Teddi’s legs wouldn’t budge.

“I’m stuck, I’m stuck,” he thought.

“What on earth should I do?”

Suddenly, a friendly hand appeared,

"Bear, we need a good shampoo."

Then, out of the sky a rope flew by,

and the kids called "1, 2, 3!"

They worked as one, together a team.

Even the littlest bee.

Friends for life, Teddi and Quinn,

from that day in the pond.

One can never tell,

what can start

a lasting bond.

“Teddi bear, Teddi bear,

what made you show such care?”

Teddi looked down at his legs and said,

"Because...it hurts when people stare."

Teddi's choice of valor,
helped keep his fears at bay.
His act began a chain of courage,
showing others a kinder way.